School Is A Nightmare #1

First Week, Worst Week

RAYMOND BEAN

ISBN: 1466220937
ISBN 13: 9781466220935

www.raymondbean.com

Other books by Raymond Bean

<u>School Is A Nightmare Series</u>
**School Is A Nightmare #2 The Field Trip
(Coming Winter 2012)**

<u>Sweet Farts Series</u>
**Sweet Farts #1
Sweet Farts #2 Rippin' It Old School
Sweet Farts #3 Blown Away
(Coming April 3, 2012)**

Interested in scheduling an author visit or web based author talk?
Email us at raymondbeanbooks@gmail.com

Contents

1
I'm Too Busy For School

If you ask me, school's a nightmare. I know you probably think your school is pretty bad, but trust me, it's nothing compared to mine. The biggest problem I have with mine is I don't want to be there. I'm a busy guy. There are about a trillion other things I'd rather be doing with my time.

My mom always says, "You'd be bored out of your mind if you didn't go to school during the day." She's wrong. If I didn't have to go to school, I'd be free to pursue my many hobbies, such as mastering my favorite video games, re-laxing on the couch, playing sports, riding my bike, skateboarding, making cartoons, playing computer games, watching TV (yeah, I consider it a hobby), and so many more. I've already got too many interests to waste my time with school.

Unfortunately for me, Mom was in full-blown back-to-school mode earlier than ever this year. All summer long she was talking about my class list and all the things she needed to buy from the store. Every time she brought school up, I covered my ears and started to hum. "Don't want to talk about it," I said. "You're destroying my summer bliss."

It never worked, of course, because both of my sisters absolutely *love* school. They're even worse than my mom. About three weeks before school was scheduled to start, on a beautiful summer Wednesday, they were arguing over who could look at the back-to-school supply catalog from the office supply store. I'm talking about a full-on tug-of-war and tears over who got to look at the new folders and notebooks on sale!

If it were up to me, I'd show up to school on the first day with nothing but my snack, my lunch, and a football to play at recess. I also wouldn't mind a pillow so I could sleep through the boring parts. The problem, of course, is it's not up to me. I'm still a kid, and when you're a kid, you just have to suck it up.

2
Shoes

The thought of going school shopping causes me major stress. I'm not a fan. When we go shopping for shoes, it's not a ten-minute trip to the store. It's hours and hours of shopping. It's never just one store. It's always lots of stores. The reason it takes so long is the girls take up most of the day deciding on their shoes. They don't get just one pair of sneakers. They get sandals, open toe, closed toe, rain boots (which must have a matching jacket), regular boots, slip-ons, slip-offs, and the list goes on.

I pride myself on picking a pair in under five seconds. If you can't pick a pair of sneakers in under five seconds, you're thinking too hard. The way I do it is I walk up to the boys' section and scan the wall once and only once. The pair that jumps out at me is the pair I pick. There is no second-guessing, no wondering if I should pick the pair next to it—no, one pick, one time, and done! I bet if I was on my own I could be out the door and wearing my new shoes in under two minutes.

But the girls and Mom have to talk about which pair they think is right for me. This year, I picked out a pair of regular skate sneakers. They were black with neon green on the bottom. They were comfortable, and they were cool. Of course, my sister had to tell Mom that William who lives down the street from us had the same pair in the spring and sprained his ankle.

"He sprained his ankle because he jumped off a six-foot-high loading dock behind the supermarket," I told Becky, who's ten and only a year older than me, but acts like my second mother. But the damage was done. I could see the worry on Mom's face.

"Why don't we try something else?" she said. "How about these?" she said holding up a pair of solid white sneakers that looked like they were made fifty years ago.

"No way, Mom," I said.

Becky and Mindy gave each other this sneaky little smile that told me they were out to convince Mom to buy me the lame sneakers. Mindy said, "Those are cool, Mom." Mindy is eleven, but thinks she's a teenager.

"They are pretty awesome," Becky added.

"Mom, they're messing with me. They don't think those sneakers are cool," I said.

"Girls, are you trying to help or make this harder than it has to be?" Mom asked.

The girls looked at Mom with their sweetest smiles and told her they just wanted to help. "Wouldn't it be a shame if Justin sprained his ankle wearing the same shoes that William was wearing?" Becky said.

"Or worse!" Mindy added. "What if he broke his neck!" She winked at me as she said it.

Mom is always worried about me breaking my neck. No matter what it is that I do, she always says, "Please be careful, Justin. I don't want you breaking your neck."

I would understand if she knew a whole bunch of people who had actually broken their necks, but she doesn't know any.

Mom said, "They look pretty sturdy. Put them on for me. Let's have a look."

I told her I didn't want to try them on, but it was too late. In her mind, it was a matter of safety. The cool sneakers were dangerous, and the white ones were going to keep me safe. I tied them up hoping she'd change her mind.

"I like them," the girls said at the same time.

"I do too," Mom added. "They have a nice strong heel. They make you look taller."

I took a few steps. They did make me taller. The heel was much bigger than on normal sneakers. "Mom," I said, "I think these are too high. I feel like I might break my neck in them."

"Nice try, Justin. These are perfect. I like the high heel. You look very sturdy on your feet."

I wondered what that even meant. How did I look sturdy on my feet? "Mom, I really feel a little wobbly in these," I said. "It's like I'm on stilts." I wasn't kidding. They were much higher than my old ones, and I kept dragging the bottoms on the ground.

"Justin, these are safer. I need to know you're safe. You said yourself that you don't care what pair you get. So I'm picking this pair for you. It's the safest pair here."

She put the pair of bright white ones in the cart and said, "We're getting these, Justin. I can't take the risk of you breaking your neck wearing those crazy trickster sneakers."

3
Supply List

Shopping for the school supply list is the purest form of torture. Unfortunately, there's no getting around this cruel ritual. Mom always takes us bright and early in the morning on the last Monday before school starts. You know how you hear about these people who go shopping at four in the morning so they can get the best shopping deals around the holidays? My mom does it with school supplies.

The store doesn't open until nine thirty on Monday, but she takes us all to breakfast at seven, and then it's a quick trip to the super-market that's right next door to the office supply place. She's usually done with her shopping around nine, and then we wait at the front door of the store until it opens.

This year it was raining a little bit. "Come on, Mom," I said, "this is crazy. We're standing in the rain so we can save a few bucks on folders!"

"You know full well that today is one-cent folder day. One-cent folder day happens once a year, and since you all need at least five folders each, I'll save about fifteen dollars on just the folders. Who knows how much I'll save on the other deals?"

"Relax, Justin," Becky said.

"You're so unappreciative," Mindy added. They shook their heads at me, and Mindy whispered loud enough for all of us to hear, "Unbelievable!"

"Give me a break, Mindy," I said. "You wouldn't be all smiles if we were on line for something I wanted to do, like go to a football game or something."

"You're right. I wouldn't be all smiles if I was on line for a football game because football is ridiculous and violent. Waiting on line with my mother so she can buy my school supplies is a privilege," Mindy said.

"Seriously! Do you know how many kids in the world don't have any school supplies?" Becky chimed in.

We argued back and forth until the doors opened. This year, Mom was calmer than usual. It was as if she had accepted that we would argue on school supply list day. All she cared about was getting those one-cent folders. She didn't seem to mind if her one and only son was tortured in the process.

By the time the doors opened, there was a line of women waiting to get in the door. I noticed most of them had the sense to leave their kids at home. Only the truly crazy people were there as a family.

Once we were inside, Mom gave us each our own list, a highlighter, and a cart. "This year," she said, "you're going to do your own school supply list shopping. You're all old enough to read the list and pick your own supplies now, so, you're on your own. I'll be waiting in the front of the store if you have any problems."

"This is soooo awesome!" Becky said.

"I know. It's like we're in college and we're living on our own," Mindy yelped.

They scurried off so fast that if they had been driving cars, the tires would have screeched.

I didn't move. "Aren't you going to go and get your supplies?" Mom asked.

"No," I said, "I don't want to."

"Justin, you have to get your supplies so you're ready on the first day."

"I don't want to be ready on the first day. I want to take this list and light it on fire."

"That's a horrible thing to say. Do you know how many kids around the world don't even have the chance to go to school?"

"Yes, I do. I wish I could give one of them my spot. In fact, I think we should do that. You're always telling us about the importance of giving. What better gift than to give a child in need the gift of education? Can't we e-mail the president and tell him I'm volunteering my spot?"

"That's very sweet, but then you wouldn't learn anything."

"Mom," I said, being as serious as I possibly could, "I know enough. I know how to read, I know how to write, and I know how to use Google! What else do I need to know?"

"You're being ridiculous. Please go pick out your supplies."

"I think we should call the White House. Think about it, the story of a boy sacrificing his education for someone less fortunate. It's beautiful!" I said. "You might even get to meet Oprah!"

"Justin, I'm losing my patience," she said.

I could tell she had lost her sense of humor and that I was pushing my luck. I wasn't kidding, though. It would be amazing if I could actually give my education away to some other kid. I'd pay the kid to go to school for me if I had the chance. If I gave my education to some needy kid, all the moms would be gushing over me and telling me what an amazing person I am. Oprah would probably give me a bunch of money, season tickets to the Jets, and I could write a book about how awesome I am.

I was picturing it all in my head when Mom shouted, "Go get your supplies!"

4
Clothes

After surviving supplies, I was about ready to hitchhike my way to Canada. In the movies, whenever some guy is trying to hide out so no one ever finds him, he heads for Mexico. I always thought that was kind of foolish because you need to know Spanish in Mexico. Since I don't speak Spanish, when I hit the road, I'm headed for Canada. They speak English and love hockey. It's perfect for me.

Mom always loves to tackle back-to-school clothes the day after back-to-school supplies

day. It's always a Tuesday, the last day before
school starts. She says there are great deals on
the last day because everyone else has already
done their shopping.

This year I was only about fifty bucks short
for a bus ticket to Canada. Maybe next year I'll
head for the border when I have enough money.
I'd rather let my sisters throw darts at me from
close range than go back-to-school clothes shopping on the last day of the summer.

It always takes my sisters about a hundred
and fifty thousand years to pick out everything,
from sweaters to socks. They try on so many
things they might as well just go into the store
and take everything off the rack and drag it to
the dressing room. Instead, they take one thing
off the rack at a time. They try it on, look in
the mirror, decide they don't like it, and go off
to get something else. By the time they're done,
the dressing rooms look like a tornado touched
down. And one of them always ends up crying.
It usually happens somewhere between picking

out their jeans and their dresses. Sometimes it's because they both want the same thing. It's endless, and I wouldn't wish it on my worst enemy.

This year I brought along *Night of the Space Face* for my game system to play while I waited. The game was brand new, I'd never played it before, and I was able to beat the entire game before they finished shopping! At one point, around two in the afternoon, I thought I might start crying, but I think I fainted instead.

"Don't be so dramatic," my mother said when I told her that we'd been in the store so long that I didn't think my friends would recognize me when I got home.

"Stop it," she scolded, "girls need more time to pick out their clothes. You should be happy you're a boy."

"I am," I said confidently. "I'm just not happy I'm a boy with two sisters. We've been in here so long, I need a shave," I tried to get Mom to feel my face for facial hair.

"Give me a break, Justin. You're going to want just as much time when we get to the boys' section."

"No, I won't. Not if you let me pick my own stuff like you did with the supplies. Just give me the list, and I'll take care of the rest."

"Okay," she said. "When the girls are done, you can pick out your own clothes this year."

I couldn't believe it. *I'll have us out of here in no time,* I thought.

When the girls were *finally* done, we went to the boys' section. I spent exactly twelve minutes picking out my clothes. I timed it. We walked in at 3:42 and were on line at 3:54. It was a personal record, and I was as happy as a clam standing on line with my pile of clothes. I couldn't wait to get home and was thinking about meeting up with the guys on the block for a game of hockey, when Becky said, "All his clothes are the same color."

My mom, who was perfectly content to let me pick my own stuff for once in my life, decided to take a closer look.

"She's right, Mom. All his clothes are green," Mindy said.

"I like green," I said. "I don't mind, and neither should all of you. You said I could pick my own stuff, Mom."

"Oh no, mister," Mom said. "You can't wear all green every day."

"It's not all green, Mom. I just picked out a bunch of things that I like."

"Honey, everything you picked is Jets clothes."

"I know," I said. *I don't see what's wrong with supporting my team every day,* I thought.

"You can't wear Jets clothes every day," Mom said. The girls were snickering behind her.

"Mom, I'm old enough to decide what to wear each day. Let me get this stuff. Please!"

"I can't allow this, honey. I'll tell you what. You can pick out one Jets shirt, and then we can get you a green collared shirt and…"

She lost me at collared shirt. I knew once the collared shirt was in the mix, my battle was lost. I could resist all I wanted. The girls and Mom were about to dress me just like they had every year before. I was about to get collared shirts, striped shirts, tight jeans, colored socks, and boxer shorts that looked like they were made for a nine-hundred-year-old man. I was like one of those dress-up dummies they use at the clothing stores, only miserable.

"We're going to make you look *fabulous,*" Mindy said.

"You're gonna love it," Becky added. She had some kind of clip in her mouth. She loves those fashion reality shows where they make clothes. They always walk around with clips in their mouths while they're making the clothes. I don't know where she got it.

"No, I'm not!" I argued.

It was too late. They were dragging me off to the dressing room. "Mom, help," I pleaded, looking back at her.

"Remember, he gets to pick one Jets shirt, girls," she reminded.

I tried to resist, but my sisters are surprisingly strong.

5
Back-to-School Eve

The last few days of summer vanish before your eyes like the sand through an hourglass. One day the summer feels like it will go on forever, and the next, it's what I like to call "Back-to-School Eve." In my opinion, Back-to-School Eve is the scariest night of the year.

This year's eve, after we got home from clothes shopping, my sisters tried on outfits in their rooms and packed supplies in their backpacks. I played video games, went outside to search for snakes for a while, and looked at my hockey cards.

I went online to check the prices for a bus ticket to Canada. I was still fifty bucks short of the seventy-three-dollar ticket. I clicked on the calculator and figured if I saved fifty cents a day for a hundred days, I'd have enough to take off in the spring.

I imagined getting on the 8:00 a.m. bus that arrived in Canada at 4:00 p.m. If I went, I'd wait until I got there and then send three letters. One would be addressed to my school, letting them know that I wasn't coming in anymore. The other would be to the president of the United States, letting him know that I didn't need my education and he could feel free to give some other kid my spot. The third letter would be to my parents, apologizing for skipping town on them.

I was completely in my fantasy when I noticed the advertisement on the bus schedule.

Brown Dog Bus Company is giving away a $100 voucher good for travel to any of our destinations. Enter to win today and get ready to hit the open road.

Click here for details.

It was fate. It was meant to be. It was destiny! The contest rules said all I had to do was enter my e-mail address and my reason for entering. I typed in the e-mail address, and then for the reason wrote: *I need to escape.*

The contest rules didn't say anything about how many times you could enter, so I kept entering and entering. I'm not sure how many times I entered, but filling out the e-mail box and my reason for getting away only took a few seconds, so I must have entered a few hundred times. My click finger was starting to hurt when Mom called me down for dinner.

"I'm soooo excited about tomorrow," Becky said.

"Me too!" Mindy added.

"Mom, can we get up early tomorrow? I love the first day so much, I want to savor the morning and be completely ready when I head to the bus stop," Becky said.

"Sure," Mom said. "We can make a great big breakfast, and you guys can make sure all your stuff is ready to go."

Dad was messing with his phone. "Dad, did you like school when you were growing up?" I asked.

"Nooo! It was like torture," Dad said without looking up.

"Don't say that," Mom scolded.

"You have to remember things were a lot different back then," he said, trying to recover. "They hit us with rulers and tied pencils to our hands."

"Dad, you went to the same school I'm going to. You even had Mrs. Cliff in fourth grade. The woman's been teaching so long she's getting the son of one of her students from the thirties," I said.

"I was not even born in the thirties, Justin, and Mrs. Cliff was all right," he lied.

"She was all right? That's not what you told me last year when you said you wanted to jump off a cliff when you had Mrs. Cliff."

"Your father never said any such thing!" my mom said.

"Yeah, he did," Becky and Mindy said at the same time.

"I was kidding. Mrs. Cliff was very nice. You're going to have a great year."

6
Cock-a-Doodle-Doo

Opening your eyes on that first day of school is like no other morning. It's the opposite of the feeling you get on your birthday. On the first day of school, my eyes opened, and I immediately shut them. I heard my sisters getting ready and smelled coffee, which meant Mom was up. It was raining. *Great*, I thought, *there goes outdoor recess!*

Dad opened my door and pulled out the huge plastic horn we got on our vacation to Vermont. It sounded like the horn on a ferry. It was so loud that when I blew it in my sister's ear on our vacation, she said she was deaf for the rest of the day. I think she was faking it a little, but it was hard to know for sure.

"Come on, Dad! Just five more minutes," I begged.

"Can't do it, kiddo. You're kind of running late already. Get up and hurry up," he said, blowing the horn long and hard.

I covered my ears and hid under the covers. "Take all the money in my bank account and do whatever you want with it. Just don't send me to school."

"You have to go to school. It's the law, and you only have about twenty bucks in your account, so it's not such a tempting offer."

"Name your price. I'll owe you the rest and pay it off when I grow up."

"Out of bed, son! I'm off to work. Have a fun day with the Cliff! Try to earn some marbles for your class."

"What do you mean?" I asked.

"You'll see," he said, pulling off my covers and giving the horn one final blow.

7
Soup Mix

I was in a rotten mood. I ran to the bathroom and slammed into the door because it was locked, which put me in an even more rotten mood. Mindy was in the shower and singing at the top of her lungs.

"Justin," my mom shouted, "your snake is loose again!"

I flew down the stairs and sprinted into the den. The cover to my boa constrictor Mr. Squeeze's cage was off again. I dropped to the floor and crawled along the front of the couch to see if he was hiding under it. He loves to get out and hide under things. The week before, I found him under the fridge. Dad had to get help from Harvey next door to help slide it out and not crush him. Mom was furious. The girls cried and told Dad they weren't safe in their own home. Mom and Dad told me if my snake got out one more time, I'd have to get rid of him.

Half my body was under the big chair in the den when Becky screamed so loud it would have stopped a train. I bolted up as if I'd been electrocuted and slammed my head hard on the wooden edge of the couch. Somehow I made it to my feet and stumbled toward the downstairs bathroom. She was blasting Mr. Squeeze with hair spray.

"Stop!" I shouted. "You're going to hurt him!"

She didn't stop. My snake was in the cabinet under the sink, and she was unloading on him.

"*Stop!*" I screamed again. "You're getting it in his eyes!"

She didn't care. She blasted away. I leaned over to grab him and accidentally knocked into her. She lost her balance and fell hands first into the toilet.

"Mom!" she shouted.

I snatched up Mr. Squeeze and ran him back to his cage, passing Mom in the hall.

"Good! You found him," she said. "That thing has to go, Justin!"

I put Mr. Squeeze back in his tank, lifted up the whole thing, and raced it up to my room. Mindy stuck her head out of the upstairs bathroom and asked me what was going on.

"Mr. Squeeze got out again and scared Becky," I said.

She smiled, pumped her fist, and said, "Yes! That thing is finally out of here."

"I'm not getting rid of him," I announced, running toward my room. I put the cage in my closet and covered it with a blanket.

I heard Mindy singing from the shower, "He's gone, oh yeah! That sliiiimeee, stinkin', no-good snake is fiiiiinally gone! Oh yeah! That sliiii-meee, stinkin', no-good snake is *gone*!"

I slammed my closet door and sprinted down to the kitchen. Mom and Becky were still in the bathroom washing her hands and being completely overdramatic. "It could have killed me," I heard her say through her tears. "I can't wait until that beast is out of our house forever!"

"I'm not giving him away!" I shouted back, grabbing a packet of French onion soup mix and racing back up the steps.

Mindy kept singing, "He's gone…"

"Cut it out!" I yelled, tearing off the top of the soup mix packet and pouring the brown powder into my hand. She kept on singing. I gave it a sniff. It smelled like a combination of beef, salt, and onions. "I'm telling you one last time, *cut it out!*" She kept on singing. I knew what I did next was going to land me in epic trouble with my parents, but it was worth it. She was begging for it. I went into the bathroom, stood on the toilet, and threw the soup mix over the curtain. Then I ran for my life.

8
We Missed the Bus, and Your Sister Smells Like Soup

I'd never actually soup-mixed a person before, but I'd heard kids talk about it. The soup mix powder mixes with the hot shower water and creates a disgusting mixture of soapy soup. The worst part is it gets in your hair, and the smell is really hard to get out. It's about as close to getting sprayed by a skunk as you can get, except you smell like soup instead of a skunk.

Mom spent about twenty minutes in the bathroom trying to help Mindy get the smell out. I sat in my room waiting for what would most likely be my death. Becky appeared in my doorway.

"What?" I asked.

"Thanks to you, we missed the bus!"

She was right. I pulled up my shade and saw the back of the bus rolling away from the house.

"Awesome!" I said.

"You're not going to think it's awesome when Mom realizes it. *Mom!* We missed the bus!" she yelled.

I heard Mom say, "You've got to be kidding me!"

Mindy cried, which made Becky cry, which made Mom cry.

By the time we all got in the car, it was 8:20. The girls were puffy-eyed and very quiet. Mom looked about as mad as I'd ever seen her. The smell of French onion soup hung thick in the air. It made me kind of hungry, and I realized I hadn't eaten any breakfast.

"You smell delicious," I said to Mindy. I was already dead. I might as well go down in a blaze of glory.

The girls didn't look at me. They were giving me the silent treatment, which was a win in my book because I didn't have to listen to them anymore.

"I can't believe you threw a pack of soup mix on your sister!" Mom said. "Where did you learn to be so aggressive?"

"Mom, she was asking for it. She was singing that I had to get rid of Mr. Squeeze."

"You do. That was the deal. We agreed the next time he got out, he was gone. Now he's gone. That thing is getting too big, and you can't contain it anymore."

"I just need a heavier lid or a bigger tank," I said.

"You won't need either because that snake is going back to the pet store today."

"Please, Mom! Give me one more chance."

"You used up your 'one more chance' this morning when that thing almost ate your sister in the bathroom."

"Can't we talk about it?" I knew it was a lost cause, but I had to try.

"Your father will bring it to the pet store on his lunch break and figure out what to do. That thing is not spending one more night in *my* house. When you get home from school, your father and I will let you know your punishment for throwing soup mix on your sister."

9
I Don't Know Anyone

I knew before I walked into Mrs. Cliff's room that I was going to hate it. Every kid I had asked about her had told me how mean she was. The kids all said that she made her class work all day long. No breaks, no games, no fun.

I had exactly zero friends in the class too. We all got our teachers' names a few days before the first day, and I immediately called everyone I knew, and not one of them was in my class.

Of course my three best friends were all in the same class and had the coolest teacher in the school, Ms. Fiesta. She gave out all kinds of snacks, had parties, and everyone wanted to be in her class. Everyone who had ever had her said she's the best. I was hoping all summer long that I'd be in her class, but that's not the way it worked out.

On my way to class, I passed Ms. Fiesta's class. I could hear music. I peeked through the door to see kids doing the limbo, wearing tropical shirts and smiling.

I walked into my class, and it felt like a prison library. No one was smiling. Mrs. Cliff said, "Good morning, Justin."

"Hi," I managed, quickly panning the room. I didn't see one friendly face. The only desk left was the one closest to Mrs. Cliff's desk. *Great,* I thought. I had to sit at the edge of the Cliff, all the way in the front.

"You can unpack your things and settle in. The class is busy writing about their favorite summer memory."

Perfect, I thought. *She's started with the most predictable first-day-of-school activity known to man. I think the first time a teacher assigned that activity, kids rode dinosaurs to school.*

"Cool," I said, heading to my desk. I dropped my backpack on the floor and plopped heavily into the seat. It was missing one of the little metal caps on the bottom of one of the legs, so it wobbled. The top of the desk had a bunch of stuff scratched in the top. There were a few names in big letters, and on the top corner it said:

YUR LAME

That's a nice welcome, I thought, unzipping my backpack. I pulled the zipper open, and it hit me: *I left all my supplies at home.* Mom had told us to load everything into our backpacks the day we went supply shopping. I took the shopping bags up to my room, but never got around to putting the stuff in my backpack.

I didn't have any supplies, but I had everything I'd brought on our trip to Vermont that summer. There was a bunch of rubber reptiles, a Wiffle ball, a foam football, a few comic books, a bunch of rocks I brought home, a moldy bathing suit, and a ziplock bag full of candy. I reached in, pretending to get my stuff while I figured out my next move.

"Is everything all right? Justin?"

"Oh yeah," I lied. "Everything is just fine. It's just that I grabbed the wrong backpack this morning. I left all my supplies at home."

Mrs. Cliff smiled, but I wasn't buying it. She was annoyed. I can always tell when an adult smiles but is really frustrated with me. She calmly walked to her desk, took a preprinted slip from a small stack of papers, and handed it to me.

"There's always one," she said. "Please bring this note home tonight and have your parents sign it. I'll expect your supplies tomorrow."

"Okay, but I have them. They're just not here."

"Exactly!" she said, not as nice this time. "And here is where we need them, isn't it?"

This is the beginning of my nightmare, I thought. 182 more days with Mrs. Cliff was going to feel like 182 million years.

"Isn't it?" she repeated.

"Yes," I said, shrugging and giving her my cutest smile. "What can you do? Stuff happens, right?"

"Yes, stuff happens. In this case, I would say that stuff did not happen. Do you have anything in that pack that you can use today?"

"I have a bunch of candy I can share," I said, trying my cute smile one more time. It didn't work.

10
How About a Summary?

Mrs. Cliff gave me a notebook and a few pencils. Then she told me that since I was late, I'd missed her explanation of the class reward system. On her desk there were three large antique-looking containers. The middle jar was full of colorful marbles. On each side of the full jar was an empty jar. One of the empty ones had a happy face on it, and the other had a sad face on it. She explained that each time a member of the class was caught doing something good, a marble was placed in the happy face, and each time someone in the class was caught doing something wrong, a marble went in the sad face.

"Normally your lack of preparation would earn the class one negative marble, but since it's the first day, I'm willing to let it go. However, the next time I will not be so forgiving."

I couldn't believe she would punish the whole class for one kid's mistake.

"Also," she continued, "under no circumstances are you to touch the marbles or any of the three jars. They are very delicate antique glass. I've had them since my very first day of teaching. I am the only one to touch them, understand?"

"Sure, no problem. I won't."

"Very good then. Let's get to work on your summer writing."

I tried to think about my summer. I loved summer more than words could say, but I didn't have *one magical moment* that I wanted to write a whole paragraph about. I decided the best thing to do was write about how I loved all of summer. It was a unique twist.

I was about four sentences in when Mrs. Cliff strolled by. She looked over my shoulder and said, "Justin, you are to select one moment from the summer that was your absolute favorite and write about that one moment. You seem to be writing about several moments."

"I am. I couldn't think of just one, so I'm giving more of a summary."

"We're not writing a summary. We are writing about one moment," she reminded me.

Oh boy, I thought. *I might as well be in cuffs. I can't even pick what to write about on the first day of school.* I didn't mind doing writing. I like writing. It was the fact that I wasn't allowed to decide for myself what to write about. I was feeling hungry and frustrated. "I didn't have any super amazing moments that were the number one moment kind of thing. I just had a great summer. I wish it had never ended."

"I suggest you pick one moment and start writing about it. We'll share in ten minutes."

The girl sitting on my left, who was picking at her teeth with a paper clip, smiled and held her hands up as if to say, *what can you do?* The girl on my right, who was in my class the year before, tapped her watch to tell me to get to work.

Why? I thought. *Why do I have to be here for the next ten months?* I started counting the days until the first three-day weekend. There was one or two at the end of September and then one sometime in October. I drew a calendar on the page to help me out.

I was counting the days and making tally marks when Mrs. Cliff said, "Okay, everyone. Please come to the rug on the side of the class, and we can have our first writing share."

11
Breakdown

The writing share didn't go very well for me. Mrs. Cliff said, "It's only nine a.m., and you've already been unprepared twice today, Justin. I do hope this is not a sign of things to come. Remember, marbles start tomorrow." Kids eyeballed me and made it clear they didn't appreciate putting the class marbles at risk.

The rest of the day was more of the same old first-day stuff. We took a math quiz, read for thirty minutes, reviewed the continents on a world map, answered a bunch of questions about ourselves, and Mrs. Cliff read us some corny book that I'd heard a hundred times before.

I don't think I cracked a smile until we started to pack up to head home. I was ready to go in no time because I had nothing to pack.

We walked out in single file, completely silent, to find our buses.

I climbed onto mine and dropped into the first seat I could find. *One day down,* I thought. It was super hot on the bus, and the windows were all up. It was only a few stops, so I knew I'd be home in no time.

My friend Aaron sat next to me. "Hey," he said, "how was your first day?"

"Boring," I said.

"Really? Mine was awesome! We played kickball, went on the computers for a while, and got to read outside. Ms. Fiesta is the best."

"I'm happy for you," I lied, turning to look out the window.

"You know that Mike and John are in my class too, right? I didn't realize it until today, but there are two kids from my baseball team in the class too. You're my only good friend in another class."

"I know. I'm alone on my own island in Mrs. Cliff's class."

"Who's in the class?"

"No one I really know. No one that I hang out with."

"That stinks!"

"Tell me about it," I said. Then I remembered that I had a huge punishment waiting for me at home. I had been so busy being miserable at school I forgot all about the soup mix mess I'd created at home. At least my sisters wouldn't be home for a few hours because they had after-school stuff.

"I think there's something wrong with the bus," Aaron said.

"Don't tell me that," I said. "I just want this day to end."

I stood up and noticed that all the other buses were leaving. Our bus driver was on his cell phone. I watched him waving his arms around and looking pretty upset. He hung up and spoke into the loudspeaker. "Quiet please, everyone. It looks like this bus is not going anywhere, so the bus company is sending another bus to take you kids home. Sit tight. The bus should be here in a few minutes."

I didn't have a watch or any way to tell time, but it felt like an eternity before he spoke again. "It looks like the bus they were sending is also having problems, so they are sending a third bus to pick you guys up."

I'm never going to get home, I thought.

12
The Punishment

By the time I finally got home, Mom was so worried that I thought she might have forgotten about the whole mess in the morning.

"I'm so happy you're finally home. I was worried sick. I talked to the school and the bus company, and they kept telling me you'd be home in twenty minutes, and that was over two hours ago."

"It was terrible, Mom," I said, laying it on a little thick. "I don't think I can get back on the bus tomorrow. It was pretty traumatic. I might need a day to recuperate. I'm pretty dehydrated. It was like a thousand degrees on that bus."

"It's the first day. Please don't start trying to get out of going in tomorrow already."

"Maybe I should head straight to my room and get some rest so I have the energy to go back tomorrow," I said, hoping to avoid a conversation about the soup mixing.

"You can relax until your father and your sisters get home."

I ran up to my room and opened my closet door. *Please let him be here,* I thought. The tank was gone. They had followed through on their promise to get rid of Mr. Squeeze. I thought for sure that they were bluffing. I had Mr. Squeeze as a pet since second grade. It wasn't fair.

I was only in my room a short time when Mom called me downstairs. Everyone was at the kitchen table waiting to talk. Becky and Mindy looked thrilled to finally learn my punishment.

"Okay, I think we all can agree that this morning did not go the way any of us hoped," Dad said. We all nodded that we agreed.

"Justin, what was going through your mind when you decided to throw soup mix on your sister?" he asked.

"I was just so mad at both of them. Becky was practically killing my snake with hair spray, and then Mindy was singing and celebrating the fact that I was going to lose my pet."

"You should lose it!" she said. "That thing was going to kill one of us sooner or later."

"It can't kill us. It's a constrictor. You act like it has venom or something."

"I don't care what it can do. I don't want to see it ever again."

"Well, congratulations, because it's already gone."

"I gave it to one of the guys I work with to hold on to for a while until we figure out what to do with Mr. Squeeze," Dad said.

I wasn't happy about it, but it was better than them giving him back to the pet store. Hope returned.

"Can I earn him back?" I asked.

"We haven't decided," Mom said. "Let's deal with one problem at a time. I think the most pressing matter right now is your punishment for that horrible behavior this morning. Have you even apologized to your sisters?"

"*No!*" they answered in unison.

"I'm sorry I soup-mixed you," I said in my most sincere voice. My parents believed in the entire family talking about punishments before giving them out. I had been in this situation before, but this was a pretty serious offense. I knew the punishment was going to be hefty.

"Your actions this morning were a combination of bad choices," Dad said. "You created the whole drama by not making sure the snake's cage was secure. Then you knocked your sister into the toilet bowl. If that wasn't enough, you invaded your other sister's privacy by going into the bathroom, and then you threw soup mix on her!"

"I didn't mean to knock her into the toilet. It was an accident," I said, an awesome accident, sure, but still an accident. "The soup thing was because I couldn't think of any other way to make her stop. She was making fun of the fact that I had to get rid of the snake. She was being really mean."

"So you decided to be really mean back to her?" Dad said.

"I guess so. I'm not saying it was right. I just reacted in the heat of the moment. I won't do it again."

"My hair smelled like soup all day long. It still does," Mindy whined.

"You're lucky it didn't get in her eyes," Becky added. "Sarah at school said she heard about a kid who was blinded by chicken noodle soup once."

"That's ridiculous," I said.

"Ask her!" she said back.

"Enough," Mom interrupted. "We're just lucky she didn't slip and break her neck."

I knew Mom couldn't resist pointing out that she could have broken her neck.

"So what is the fitting punishment for a premeditated soup mixing?" Dad said, trying to be funny.

"It's not funny," Mindy pleaded.

"I'm just trying to lighten the situation, honey. What do you think his punishment should be?"

"He should lose his video games and TV forever, and he should be grounded until next summer."

"Right," I said.

"I think he's already paid a pretty big price by losing his snake. But I agree there needs to be something else."

"How about we get to do it to him?" Becky suggested.

"*Yes!*" Mindy said, perking up.

"No," Mom said, "we can't do that."

"I don't know," Dad said. "I think it might be a fitting punishment."

"You're going to let her throw soup mix on me in the shower?"

"I was thinking more along the lines of in the backyard. Go get your bathing suit and a spoon, son. You're about to get a taste of your own medicine. Mindy, go pick out the soup of the day. I'll go get the hose."

13
Tacos, Anyone?

Standing in the backyard in my bathing suit, I couldn't help thinking that Dad wasn't going to go through with it. He was probably trying to scare me and teach me a lesson. But when Mindy came out with a packet in hand, I knew it was about to go down.

"We're out of soup mix," Mom said, "so she chose taco mix. Are we sure we want to do this?"

"Yes, he had no problem throwing soup mix on his sister this morning. Why should he mind getting the same treatment?"

Becky loved it. She pulled out a beach chair and even made herself an iced tea. She tried to videotape it, but Mom told her to shut it off.

Dad turned the hose on and handed it to my sister. *I get it now,* I thought, *he's testing her. He's going to give her the hose and give her the chance to get me back, and she'll realize how mean that would be and forgive me.* Dad was pretty smart.

Only, the exact opposite happened. She unloaded on me with the icy spray from the hose, and before I knew it, I was covered head to toe in bright red taco mix powder.

It was one of the strangest moments of my life. No one knew what to do or say as I stood there stinking like a beef taco. I finally broke the silence when I said, "I forgot all my supplies today, and I'm kind of in trouble with Mrs. Cliff. I almost cost the class two marbles."

"Wonderful," Mom said, "just wonderful."

14
Viva la Shower

I couldn't wait to take a shower. Being covered in taco mix was pretty gross. It was super smelly and really hard to get off. I smelled like the school cafeteria on Taco Tuesdays.

I tried to get out of the shower as fast as possible because I thought the girls might try to give me another helping.

After my shower I went to my room and put all my school supplies into my backpack. Then I went downstairs. "What's for dinner?" I asked Mom.

"I planned on making a meat loaf, but I'm suddenly out of French onion soup mix, so I thought we would have tacos in your honor."

"I'm not really in the mood," I said.

15
Day Two

Thursday morning meant the first morning bus ride of the year. Mom made sure we didn't miss the bus. She had us all up, showered, fed, and ready to go at seven. The bus didn't come until eight! I walked outside to get the garbage cans, and it was already about ninety degrees. I was sweating from dragging the two cans up my driveway.

Mom was outside watering her flowers. "Can't I just take the day off?" I asked. "I'm still pretty upset from yesterday and last night. I think that taco mix might have given me some kind of a fever."

"Come on. You're not the only kid that has to go to school, you know. Plenty of kids don't want to go, but they make the best of it. You can't spend the rest of your life raising snakes and playing video games."

Why not? I thought. It sounded like a pretty good life to me. "I think I could. We can give it a try and see how I like it."

"Part of your problem with school is you don't give it a chance. I think they could be handing out free money and you'd complain that you didn't have any room for it in your school bag," she said.

"I wouldn't mind some free money. But you can't pay me enough to actually enjoy it. And there isn't enough money in the world to make me want to ride the bus."

"I used to love the bus growing up," she said. "My bus driver was a cute little woman named

Ms. Harc. She was the sweetest lady you could ever imagine."

"That's great for you, but I don't have Ms. Harc. I would welcome Ms. Harc, whoever she is, because my guy's crazy."

"He's not crazy! He's a nice man who drives the bus. You really need to be more appreciative. You're attitude is too negative."

"I'm negative for a reason, trust me. The bus is like a nightmare. Every time it rolls up to the bus stop, I feel like it's going to just open its mouth and eat one of us."

"You are so dramatic, Justin. It's a ten-minute ride to the school. How bad can it be?"

In truth, the bus wasn't really that bad. It was the fact that once I got on, the next place I got off was school. I like being home. It's where I keep all my stuff, and I can chew gum.

16
Oh Man!

The kids at my bus stop were the same as the year before. Becky and Mindy were hanging out under the big tree on Mrs. Minihan's lawn. Me and the Conisi brothers stood by the fire hydrant, where we always did. One time we found a turtle on the grass right behind the fire hydrant. Every time I went to the bus stop, I secretly hoped to find it again.

"Why weren't you on the bus yesterday?" one of the brothers asked.

"Don't ask."

"We thought you moved or something," the other brother said.

"Nope, I'm thinking about moving to Canada, though."

"I heard in Canada everything costs less than it does in the U.S. If you have a dollar, it's like having two dollars!"

I listened to him tell all about Canada and how much more our money is worth there. If he was right, it meant that once I was there, my money would be worth double.

Up the block, brakes squeaked. I took a deep breath. The girls giggled and high-fived each other. "Oh man," I complained.

"What's the matter?" the younger one asked. "Are you afraid?"

"No, I just wish I could stay home. Why would I want to go to school when I could spend the day playing at home?"

"He's afraid," the older one said. I tried to convince them that I wasn't afraid, but it was too late. "Hey, Becky and Mindy, did you know your brother is afraid of the bus?" he called.

"I'm not afraid of the bus," I defended. "I just don't want to go to school. Why is everyone so surprised that I don't like school? Am I the only one that has other things I'd rather be doing?"

"I have a million things I'd rather be doing, but kids have to go to school. There's no sense in wishing you didn't have to go because there's no way out of it," the older one said.

If I hop a bus to Canada, I'd be out of it, I thought. I imagined getting off the bus in Canada. I wondered if it was true that every dollar you had was worth two up there. I remembered my dad one time talking about how the dollar was stronger in Canada. If I saved one hundred dollars, it would be worth two hundred in Canada. I was daydreaming about living the good life in Canada when I heard the low roar of the bus engine getting louder. Then I saw it.

"Oh man," I whispered.

"You are afraid," one of the brothers said again.

17
He's Afraid

Mindy and Becky were the first ones on the bus. All the other kids lined up and looked pretty happy to be on their way to school. I kind of wished I was more like them. If I liked school, my life would be pretty easy.

The bus doors flew open like a giant mouth ready to swallow us up. The bus driver wasn't the crazy guy I had on the way home the day before. It was a lady with huge curly hair and big round glasses. They were the thickest glasses I'd ever seen.

Everyone climbed on, and I stood at the bottom of the steps and thought about running for it.

"Come on, young man," she said. "I have a seat right up here behind me. You don't have to be afraid."

I heard giggles from some of the other kids. On my way up the steps, I tripped because of my huge heels.

"Take it slow, little fella," she said as if I was in kindergarten.

"I'm fine," I said.

She waved her hand to signal that she wanted me to come closer. I leaned in. "Your sisters told me that your mom wants you to sit right behind me because you're scared of the bus. Don't worry, little buddy. You're going to be just fine."

I made eye contact with the girls, who were sitting all the way in the back. Mindy winked, and Becky blew me a kiss. I turned back to the driver. "My mom didn't say that I had to sit in the front."

She winked at me. "Okay, big fella. You just sit there because *you* want to."

"I don't want to sit there," I said clearly. It was no use. She was already convinced that my mom wanted me in the front seat behind the driver, and that's where I sat.

18
Day Two

I tripped going down the steps too. The heels on my shoes were so big I felt like I was on stilts. I was the second kid into the class. Mrs. Cliff was at her desk, polishing the jars. I couldn't tell if she realized I was in the room, but then she said, "Are we prepared today, Justin?"

"Yep!" I said.

She put down her polishing rag and walked to my desk. "We do not say 'yep.' We say 'yes' in this class. 'Yep' is going in the graveyard. Please go fill out a cutout of a tombstone and write 'yep' on it."

In the corner, by the closet, was a bulletin board of a spooky-looking graveyard. The title of the billboard read: These Words Are Put to Rest. It gave me a creepy feeling. I couldn't believe a teacher would put something like that up. I wrote the "yep" on the tombstone cutout and taped it to the board.

"Thank you, Justin," she said. "Do you have your supplies today?"

"Yes," I said.

"Excellent! Today is a fresh start. Please get unpacked, and let's get to work." I walked to my desk and started putting away my supplies. She walked over to my desk and said, "Good job."

I smiled. *Maybe she wasn't so bad after all,* I thought.

Then she said, "I see that we have the same taste in shoes."

"What do you mean?" I asked.

She lifted her leg a little and pointed to her sneakers. They were the same exact pair as mine. I almost fell out of my seat.

I faked a smile and weakly said, "Cool."

19
Smashed

The rest of the morning was alright, but it was taking forever. Time seemed to slow down at school. Five minutes felt like an hour. An hour felt like a day. When recess finally rolled around, I couldn't wait to get outside. I watched the clock like a hawk for the final minutes to click away.

When it was time, I jumped up and announced, "Recess! It's time for recess!"

Mrs. Cliff was at her desk, and the look on her face told me she didn't appreciate the interruption. She stood and walked to the center of the room. "I'm aware of the time, Justin. Students in my class do not stand and shout whenever they feel like it. I'm sorry to inform you that you are the first student to cost the class a marble. Please go take one marble from the center jar and place it in the sad-face jar."

I thought she was being a little harsh. It was time for recess. I think she was annoyed that I caught her mistake. We would have been late for recess if I hadn't said anything.

The class lined up as I walked over to her desk to move the marble. I must have been rushing to get it in the jar and get outside because the next thing I knew, I was falling. It all happened in slow motion. The heel on my right sneaker scraped the floor, and then my left sneaker bonked off the leg of someone's desk. I wobbled for a second and almost caught my balance, but it was too late. I landed right on Mrs. Cliff's desk, crashing right into the jars. They launched across her desk and catapulted off the other side. The empty happy-face jar hit the floor like a bomb, and glass went in every direction. The sad-face jar hit Mrs. Cliff's coffee mug. Her coffee spilled onto her desk, and the jar broke apart, sending glass across her papers and plan book. The middle jar with all the marbles looked like it might survive, but then a piece of one of the other jars clanked it, sending a crack running up the side. When the crack reached the top, the jar collapsed, and hundreds of colored glass marbles spilled out onto the floor. Each one shattered as it hit. It was like a mini fireworks show.

When it finally stopped, I was holding myself up on Mrs. Cliff's desk. My hands were in a puddle of hot coffee. It was a miracle that I wasn't cut.

"I'm okay," I said.

"I'm not sure about that," Mrs. Cliff said.

20
Payback

When I got home, Mom and Dad already knew all about the smash job I had done on Mrs. Cliff's behavior jars. "What were you thinking?" Mom asked. We were in the yard, sitting at the table.

"I didn't do anything wrong. It was these sneakers. I'm lucky I didn't break my neck."

"That's a little dramatic," Mom said.

"Mom, I fell getting on the bus, I fell getting off the bus, and I fell walking in class. I'm lucky I made it home in one piece."

"I don't think it's the shoes. They are nice and sturdy. Maybe you're walking lazy."

"Walking lazy? What does that even mean?"

"Maybe you're not lifting your feet all the way. You just need a little time to get used to them."

Dad, who had been silent the whole time, finally said, "I can't believe you broke the jars. She's had those forever. Do you know they're antiques?"

"I know. She told me all about it. Her mother was a teacher and used them in her class. She gave them to Mrs. Cliff as a gift when she became a teacher."

"This is horrible," Mom said.

"You're going to have to replace them," Dad said.

"It was an accident," I reminded them.

"It may have been an accident, but you still broke them. Replacing them is the right thing to do. It's going to have to come out of your savings."

Great, I thought, *now I'll never get to Canada.*

Dad got out his computer, and we looked online for jars that looked like Mrs. Cliff's. After about an hour of looking, we found three jars that were pretty similar. We also found a set of old-fashioned glass marbles that looked pretty close to the ones I broke. The marbles and jar, together with shipping, cost forty-five dollars. I only had twenty-three in my savings account, so Mom and Dad paid the difference and said I owed them the rest.

21
Friday!

That night I fell to sleep pretty early. I couldn't wait for the first week to be over. The bus driver made me sit behind her again because I forgot to have Mom write a note saying I didn't have to sit in the front. I didn't even mind so much because I had one thing on my mind, and that was getting to the weekend. That's the beauty of Fridays: no matter how bad your week is, you know the next day is Saturday. And Saturdays mean freedom.

I gave Mrs. Cliff the apology Mom and Dad made me write. I told them I had apologized at school, but they made me write it anyway. I also explained that I had bought new jars and they'd arrive in the mail in a few days. She seemed like she was still pretty mad, but she said thank you, and we got on with our day.

Mrs. Cliff told the class that she would keep track of behavior on paper until the new jars arrived. I was surprised that she accepted the jars. If I were the teacher, I wouldn't make a kid spend all his money to pay for something that was clearly an accident.

Mrs. Cliff said, "It's a very nice gesture, Justin, even though they can never *truly* be replaced."

I feel the same way about my savings account, I thought.

Friday went by pretty quick. It was a normal day. After the soup mix incident and the jar disaster, it was nice just to have no major problems.

At the end of the day, Mrs. Cliff handed out permission slips for our first field trip. *Nice,* I thought, *a whole day out of school!* It was exactly what I needed, something to look forward to. The slip said the trip was scheduled for the following Friday. I was psyched because it was a trip to New York City. The trip included the Statue of Liberty, Times Square, and the Brooklyn Bridge. If that wasn't cool enough, it said we were going to share a bus with Ms. Fiesta's class. *Awesome,* I thought, *I can hang out with my friends.* It was the perfect end to a perfectly awful week.

Of course, I couldn't have known then that it would be the worst field trip of my life.

Look for the next book in the series
School Is a Nightmare #2
The Field Trip
Sign up for an email alert when the next book
is released at
www.raymondbean.com

Made in the USA
Charleston, SC
10 January 2016